MW00979902

DRIFTWOOD SAVES THE WHALES

The Driftwood Saga:

Driftwood Ellesmere

Driftwood's Crusade

Driftwood Saves the Whales

Coming Soon:

Driftwood & the Necessary Forest

Driftwood's War

DRIFTWOOD SAVES THE WHALES

Volume Three in the Driftwood Saga

JAMES DAVIDGE
ILLUSTRATIONS BY ERIC JORDAN

BAYEUX

DRIFTWOOD SAVES THE WHALES: *Volume Three in the Driftwood Saga*
Copyright © 2008 James Davidge, *text;* Eric Jordan, *illustrations;* Fiona Staples, *cover illustration*

Published by: Bayeux Arts, Inc., 119 Stratton Crescent SW, Calgary, Canada T3H 1T7, www.bayeux.com

Cover image: Fiona Staples
Illustrations: Eric Jordan

Library and Archives Canada Cataloguing in Publication

Davidge, James, 1973-
    Driftwood saves the whales / James Davidge.

(Driftwood saga ; #3)
ISBN 978-1-897411-01-8

    1. Whales--Juvenile fiction. I. Title. II. Series: Davidge, James, 1973-
Driftwood saga ; #3.

PS8607.A78D7425 2008   jC813'.6
C2008-905984-0

First Printing: October 2008
Printed in Canada

Books published by Bayeux Arts/Gondolier are available at special quantity discounts to use as premiums and sales promotions, or for use in corporate training programs. For more information, please write to Special Sales, Bayeux Arts, Inc., 119 Stratton Crescent SW, Calgary, Canada T3H 1T7.

The publishing activities of Bayeux/Gondolier are supported by the Canada Council for the Arts, the Alberta Foundation for the Arts, and by the Government of Canada through its Book Publishing Industry Development Program.

Dedicated to my nephews:
Kevin, Peter and Joshua

Special Thanks to Christa Mayer, Natalie Norcross, Laurie Harris, Judd Palmer, Jason Howse, Lucy Koshan, Michael Lane, Ashis Gupta, Steve Kenderes, Rico, The Old Trout Puppet Workshop and to all my family; near, extended, speculative and imagined.

CHAPTER ONE

THE BEGINNING HUNT

Seven days ago, on her first try of the season, Driftwood built the perfect igloo.

It had a pristine shape. The arc that the dome formed was optimally constructed. Each block was of uniform thickness and supported the others around it. It spiraled up in an organic yet organized fashion. She had built in two windows made of clear ice. Her bed was just a bit bigger than needed, the ideal size. There was plenty of room for both her and her pet, Edie. Seal oil burned in a carved-out whale jawbone to maintain the home at a comfortable temperature.

Driftwood had enjoyed her time in Aujuittuq since returning to arctic Ellesmere Island. Her most recent adventure had left her feeling distraught with the rest of the world. She was finding solace in tending to her own basic needs. Her intent to hunt had become an act of distraction.

Over the course of the last week, Driftwood had become quite adept at throwing a spear. With weapon in hand, seven days after building her icy home, she was tracking her first seal. It had taken hours of quiet patience and focused analysis of her snowy surroundings. As she watched from behind an ice-frosted boulder, a large seal rolled on the frozen floor while it devoured a recently caught fish. As quietly as possible, Driftwood stood up and stretched the shaft of the spear behind her. She made sure that it was parallel to her ear and took steady aim.

I can do this, Driftwood told herself. *Be*

the spear.

She swung her arm forward, releasing her weapon just as her hand was as far in front of her as possible. The spear flew away from her in the absolute direction of the unaware seal. Driftwood watched intently.

The seal kept eating. It also appeared to be scratching its back on the ice. It seemed quite content, completely oblivious to the missile coming at it. As Driftwood continued to track the path of her throw, something unexpected happened.

The spear's path suddenly and totally changed direction. In fact, it turned completely around. Driftwood was shocked by what she saw. She was so stunned that she almost didn't react to the pointed object that was suddenly flying at her. She ducked just as her weapon flew over her and impaled a pile of snow.

Unfazed by the anomaly, she reached behind her and grabbed the spear for another try. Throwing it with unerring accuracy, she kept close eye on its path. Once again the projectile changed direction and began to soar straight up. It arched towards Driftwood and descended upon her.

Driftwood moved to the left and allowed the spear to stick in the ground. She wiggled her weapon free and held it tightly with both hands. She ran towards the seal and let out a screeching battle cry.

"Aiiiiieeee!" she yelled as she lunged at the blissful beast. About one metre before reaching her target she was bounced away. She landed on her back and found herself slightly winded, struggling to get air into her lungs.

It has some sort of protection field, Driftwood thought as she caught her breath.

"Who on Earth would be protecting a seal that's from the most isolated place in the world?" she spoke aloud.

"Who do you think?" responded a voice that Driftwood immediately recognized.

Out past where ice gives way to the Arctic

Ocean was a giant mermaid with her fish tail perched on a supernatural geyser of water. With a fingerless hand she waved at the young Driftwood.

"Sedna!" cried out Driftwood.

"Hello, my child, it is good to see you," responded the sea goddess of the Inuit, "but do not come out here as the ice is quite thin. Now tell me, dear one, how are you?"

"I've had a few adventures since I last saw you."

"I have heard this from my sister, Yemaya of the Atlantic waters, as well as from other mystical beings. You have truly traveled the world and done much good."

"Not that much," Driftwood bluntly corrected.

"What do you mean?" asked Sedna.

"It's just that for all the good I do, it seems like evil is still everywhere. It feels unstoppable."

"I've heard that you recently said you were just getting started."

"Where did you hear that?"

"From a squirrel god that overheard you at that camp you have been spending so much time at."

"Camp Magee. Squirrel god?"

"Yes."

"I don't know if I like the idea of you gods and goddesses talking about me so much."

"When you've been around as long as us, talking is one of the few things we still have the desire to do."

"Talking and keeping me from getting my dinner."

"You were trying to kill the Immortal Seal whose death shall never happen."

"The Immortal Seal?"

"Do you recall the story of how I lost my fingers?"

"Of course. Clara used to tell it to me all the time. To lighten his boat during a fierce storm, your father cut off your fingers to keep you from holding on. The tips became the seals of the Arctic."

"Ten seals," clarified Sedna, "that became the first of my kingdom. The second bones became walruses and the last of my fingers became the whales. These thirty animals gave me purpose as I became the sea goddess of the Inuit. They distracted me from the betrayal of my father. However, they too would soon become victims of the habits of man."

"What do you mean?"

"I watched as my children gave birth to the next generation of ocean creatures. I felt joy as these families of seals, walruses and whales thrived in the harsh waters of my land. My elation was thwarted by the actions of the very tribes that worshipped me. One by one, the beings that came directly from my own flesh were hunted and killed, leaving their offspring to fend for themselves until it was their turn to become the prey.

"One seal of all my original animals had managed to stay alive. She had come from the little finger of my left hand. I decided to invest some of my energy into ensuring that no harm would ever come to this creature. The laws of nature and the ways of man would not destroy my last child. Thus was created the Immortal Seal."

"It must be easy being a goddess," commented Driftwood.

"Pardon me?" responded Sedna as her geyser throne got taller. "What do you mean by that?"

"Keeping a seal alive forever and ever. Gossiping with deities from all over. Yet never really taking on the problems of the world. Must feel good being so great and not doing much about it."

"You dare suggest that it is easy being like me? Do you have any idea of the knowledge and curses I bare?"

"Obviously not, but I have read a whole encyclopedia set twice. My father is heartless, Grandfather Wood is abusive and my mother is dead. During the last few months I have much fought the nastiness of things in the form of chimera beasts and supermarket-vomiting giants. I have freed children from the slavery of chains and video games. I'm a sixteen year old girl and I've done more to make the world a better place than the combined efforts of all the magical beings I've met."

"Your selfish perspective is troublesome, angry mortal. Perhaps you need to see what I can see. I am about to give you an experience that will both enlighten and overwhelm your senses. For enduring this momentary shift in sight you will be granted a power that will increase your communication with nature. Use it well."

"What do you mean by all that?"

Sedna's eyes began to glow a blinding shade of red. A surge of energy emitted from her pupils. It traveled quickly across the surface of the ice and struck Driftwood. Instead of knocking her down, the energy caused Driftwood to levitate about two metres off the ground. Her eyes opened wide uncontrollably. Both of her pupils started to glow a bright crimson colour as they expanded to nearly fill their respective irises.

Sedna dove back into the ocean and declared, "Let's see if knowing the world as a goddess will illuminate your outlook."

CHAPTER TWO

MUCH TOO MUCH INFORMATION

Driftwood experienced a rush of static. Her head buzzed with indecipherable hums and crackles. A kaleidoscope of light and dark flickered around her. All around her. She saw sparks at the bottom of her brain and shadows from the hair on the back of her neck. After a few seconds, her vision cleared up enough for her to realize something.

She could see everything.

She saw all of Ellesmere Island, from the range of the Sawtooth Mountains to her small igloo where Edie the Eaderion was playing with a sock. The magical beast, that was parts eagle, spider and lion, was pecking at the threads with her beak while pawing the sock's toe with two of her eight feline legs. Her little wings waved frantically. In the nearby village of Aujuittuq she could see Clara, the woman who had raised Driftwood as her own, reading a book in the Kunuk family home. She was also able to look farther north to see Wilson, the cook of the Toque and Mitt Inn, the one hotel at the Eureka Research Station and the place Driftwood called home for most of her life. All alone in the Toque, he was boarding up some of the windows for the long, entirely dark winter ahead.

Her awareness drifted up to the Alert Military Outpost situated on the northern coast of Ellesmere Island. She had never been there before but she could now see soldiers working at their classified computer terminals. She was able to hear the soldiers talking. It was hard to make out what they were saying as she could still hear Wilson hammering in

Her head buzzed with indecipherable hums and crackles.

nails and Clara reading her book. Even the turning of the pages created noise that she could register.

"Trouble again at Hans Island," one of the soldiers said before Driftwood got distracted from Wilson yelling after whacking his thumb.

Hearing the word *Hans* made Driftwood indirectly think of her father. She had last seen Hans Blekansit just over a week ago in New York City when she had turned him into a rabbit. Suddenly, as she levitated, she could see him again. For the last nine days, Hans had taken refuge behind a dumpster at the back of Great Blekansit Product's corporate headquarters and mostly been living off of thrown out paper coffee cups. He was still a rabbit and Driftwood could not deny that it made her feel happy to see her diabolical dad still in his bunny state. However, she also could not deny that she was feeling much more than one mere emotion.

She was sensing everyone else's emotions.

She could feel Hans' fury as he nibbled on a hotdog bun. It was overwhelming and mostly directed at her. With every gnaw he angrily repeated two words to himself – *revenge* and *daughter*.

She became aware of someone else feeling basically the same wrathful hatred. It was her half brother, Harry, whom she had just met a few weeks earlier. She had turned him into a moonstone statue shortly after their first encounter. Harry was no longer a statue but had been sitting basically still in the Grand Cayman Islands. He hadn't left the toilet in almost a month due to a potion that Driftwood invented that had made him continuously fart which had caused him to find refuge in his washroom. Over time, it had become easiest to have food, medicine and entertainment brought to him by the servants of Blekansit Manor while he tried to work things through. Many doctors had attempted to stop the release of gas but to no avail. Driftwood could feel Harry's furious embarrassment. And his distinct discomfort. She even grasped moments of sincere reflection.

Her visions grew to include the Wood family home in Emporia, Kansas. Eva Wood had died giving birth to Driftwood. Shortly after meeting her father, Driftwood had been reunited with Eva's parents, brother and nephew. Driftwood's cousin, Del Wood, was in his room, playing his guitar and writing a song about how he broke his legs working at the local Blekan-Mart. She could feel his confusion over the future. Del wanted to play guitar for the rest of his life but did not know how to do that in Emporia. He was craving experience.

Her attention drifted to Uncle Chuck, who was in the study looking over unpaid bills. She could feel his fear that the Blekan-Mart would drive his small hardware store out of business. If things didn't turn around he was going to have no choice but to go and work for Blekan-Mart, as selling tools was the only thing Chuck knew how to do.

Her grandmother, Anne Wood, was preparing supper in the kitchen. Driftwood could feel the enormous love that Grandma Wood had for everyone around her. This love comforted Driftwood as more and more images were coming to her. When she saw Rotton Wood, her grandfather, she could barely sense his emotion as she became wrought with her own anger. Rotton had regularly beaten Driftwood's mother. This was one of the reasons Eva Wood had fled her family to die while giving birth on Ellesmere Island. Driftwood was able to feel her grandfather's denial and loneliness and his fractured emotions filled her with sorrow.

She began to think of her other grandfather and instantly she could see him as well. Heinz Blekansit, also known as Hermit the Laughing Man, was in St. John's, Newfoundland fighting alongside his two oldest friends for the first time in years. Driftwood drew comfort from Hermit's joy.

Murph Magee held onto Hermit's long beard as they flew on flying newspaper around the two sides of a giant's leg. They had caused the corporate goliath to lose his balance and begin to stumble. Driftwood was in tune with Murph's excitement.

The giant, named Jones, was created by some malevolent monks who were aiding her father's business. Jones was one of many magically mutated and enlarged office workers who tromped around the globe, consuming any resource they could find while puking out whole Blekan-Marts. Murph and Hermit were joined by Old Bart, the man who had been the closest thing to a father in Driftwood's life. He was sitting on a nearby hill and scratching his nose. The clouds above them began to darken. Old Bart let out a bellowing sneeze. Just as Bart's nose went into his other hand did lightning strike Jones. The giant stopped moving and appeared stunned by the blast. His tie was on fire. Driftwood tried to read what Jones was feeling. She sensed nothing but an encompassing numbness. The colossus fell over.

The three men congratulated each other on their victory. Their handshakes and hugs were rudely interrupted by a foot that was roughly the size of large truck. The wizards had not realized that Andrews had been traveling with Jones. The heal stamped out Hermit. The arch was enough to fell Old Bart. Murph was crushed by the huge little toe. Driftwood could actually feel the bones of her mentors break. She wanted to go and help them but she just couldn't stop taking everything in.

She began to think of her Camp Magee friends and hoped to embrace their youthful emotions to distract her from the tragedy she had just observed.

Clover was in Vancouver sitting in a Philosophy of Ethics course. She was trying to focus on learning the differences between Platonic and Socratic value systems but found herself instead fantasizing about shopping.

In another building of the University of British Columbia campus sat Clover's brother, Wave. He was trying with all his might to pay attention to a lecture on the more subtle nuances of the Periodic Table of Elements. Instead he just felt like surfing. Driftwood was experiencing Wave's Hang-Ten daydream. Just as a significant amount of drool fell from Wave's mouth onto his notebook did Driftwood then become aware of Glacier at the nearby Camp Magee.

In a thick part of the forest, Glacier was leading a game of camouflage with a large group of kids. The campers were all hiding as he held up three fingers in the air. The children had to try to see how many fingers their leader was holding up while staying unseen by him. Only two campers, named Jake and Charlotte, succeeded in the trial. Just as quickly had the game ended did Glacier yell, "Camouflage!" to again instigate another mad scurrying into the bush. Driftwood sensed Glacier relax as he took a few moments break from his twenty-four hour a day job of mass kid care.

At the archery range were Rose, Lichen and the rest of the campers. Lichen was teaching the older kids how to fire at a bull's-eye with her most commanding voice. Beside the range, Driftwood's best friend, Rose, was carefully shooting an arrow far into the open field while the younger children chased after it. Driftwood felt nostalgic for the camp. She was happy that it was now running all year round. Murph Magee was financing his family's camp with gold taken from her father. Seeing Rose gave Driftwood strength as she took on seeing even more of the world.

Driftwood's quintessential awareness traveled far away to her last two friends from Camp Magee. On the deck of an ancient and massive ship, in the middle of the Norwegian Sea, were Stormy and Tide. Stormy was a strange and brilliant boy. Tide had been a person of interest in Driftwood's life for some time. Tide had recently joined Stormy for a working vacation in Norway on a fishing boat. The two boys were withstanding a torrential downpour, a powerful gale and rocky sailing to be at the turret of a giant harpoon gun. Driftwood couldn't help but notice how cute Tide looked even when he was terrified and yelling quite desperately to Stormy.

"Don't do it!" screamed Tide as tears ran down his face.

"But I have to!" cried Stormy with a wavering voice. "The captain has ordered it!"

"The captain is a one-eyed tyrant!"

"Don't speak of Captain Odin that way!"

Stormy proceeded to punch Tide in the face. Tide stumbled to the ground and struggled to stand up as waves and rain pushed him from all directions. He frantically looked up to see Stormy grabbing the handle of the gun and aiming it out to sea. The tears that Stormy was now also shedding were being quickly washed away from the tempest's efforts.

"Forgive me," he wept as he pulled the trigger.

Moments later, Driftwood could hear a haunting yowl from the victim of Stormy's shot. She recognized the wounded creature immediately.

When Driftwood had fled her father's island a month ago, she had ridden home to Ellesmere Island on the back of a whale. After dropping Murph and Rose, her comrades of escape from Blekansit Manor, off at Camp Magee, the whale had made its way back across the Arctic Ocean into the Norwegian Sea and had recently been spotted and stalked by the Asgard, the fishing ship that Tide had joined Stormy on.

The whale's trauma caused Driftwood's awareness to seek refuge off of the planet. She started to explore the expansive and reactive activity of the entire universe.

As Stormy watched his prey thrash and weaken he felt the strong hand of the ship's first-mate squeeze his shoulder.

"Good shot, lad," affirmed the first-mate. "My hammer could not have done better. With such grand accuracy you may be spared the laughter of others."

"Thank you, Thor," Stormy said as the wind overpowered his words. "That gives me some comfort against what feels like the horrible sin I've just commited."

Thor grabbed Stormy and shook the teenager with vigor. He then handed the boy a large mug.

"Drink this mead to ease your guilt and be thankful for each and every day that the harpoon spares you, young man. We all fall victim to the final joke sooner or later."

Tide was still bouncing around unable to find his step. The whale's still corpse was being slowly reeled in by a mechanical winch.

"By the gods," whispered Stormy with his first sip.

"Exactly," confirmed Thor.

CHAPTER THREE

ANCIENT LEGENDS

Before working at Camp Magee, Stormy was raised as Anders Mikkelson in a small town in Saskatchewan called Strongfield. His grandfather, Scot Mikkelson, had immigrated there from Norway many years ago. His father, Erik Mikkelson, had been a pilot in the Canadian Forces at the nearby military base in Moose Jaw. When Anders was only five, Erik was killed when his plane was shot down during a NATO war game training exercise. The official cause of death had been listed as friendly fire.

That term bothered Anders from the moment he heard it.

Anders' mother, Danica Mikkelson, worked very hard to feed, clothe and shelter her only child. She was given much support from her father-in-law who helped in many ways to raise the boy.

One of Stormy's favorite memories of his grandfather was when he would tell old Norse legends. He had a particular recollection of hearing many stories on a cold afternoon while looking out onto the ice-covered fields which provided suitable atmosphere to the tales.

"Long ago," Scot began, "the lands of Norway were ruled by warrior gods of great power.

"Odin was the All-Father of the Norse, who called themselves the Æsir. He was a king of battle and all who died while fighting became one with him. Odin went by many names and it is from him that the word Wednesday has come about. In a quest to gain knowledge over everything, he sacrificed one eye to the old god Mímir in exchange for a drink from Mímir's

mystical well. The all-knowing All-Father ruled over his children and the other gods using an equal measure of force and trickery."

"He gave up his eye?" Anders responded with disbelief.

"Plucked it like an apple from a tree."

"Weird. Why did he do that?"

"In the land of the blind," Scot answered cryptically, "the one-eyed man is king."

Anders giggled when he heard his grandfather's explanation.

"The bravest of Odin's sons was Tyr, the god of war," Scot continued. "Tyr was unstoppable at combat and a hero who would sacrifice himself over others without hesitation. There once was a great wolf called Fenrir, who was a monstrous beast. The gods of the Æsir dared the wolf to be wrapped by a simple ribbon. The wolf did not want to seem scared but did not trust the gods. To convince Fenrir of the innocence of the dare, Tyr offered to put his right hand in the wolf's mouth. Fenrir agreed to the terms, although his earlier mistrust was well-founded. The ribbon had been magically empowered by dwarves to trap the mighty wolf. In exchange, Fenrir bit off Tyr's hand."

"These gods sure lost a lot of body parts."

"They were violent times."

"Aren't they still, Grandpa?" Anders asked as he reflected on his father's death in the armed forces. "Don't we still live in stupidly violent times?"

"I'm afraid so."

Anders listened intently as the tales continued.

"The mightiest of Odin's children was Thor, God of Thunder and Thursday. Using Mjöllnir, his legendary hammer, he struck down many a giant of both the frost and mountain variety. Odin was worshipped by the noblemen of Norway but Thor's feats made him a god worshipped by the slaves. Thor had the highest stature in Asgard yet he was also incredibly boastful and despised being laughed at."

"Sounds like the bullies at my school," commented Anders.

"Baldar was a god of the most pure and beautiful nature, a great warrior yet ever resplendent in innocence. The positive opinion concerning Baldar's appearance made him quite vain which led to nervousness for his well-being. All of Asgard was panicked whenever Baldar had dreams of his own death. It was believed by many that his murder would bring about Ragnarok, the Norse word for the end of days. Due to this, no one would ever try to harm him except the most dangerous god of the Norse."

"Who's that?"

"Loki, a trickster god, who was able to manipulate his situations to appear to be friend to both the Æsir and the giants alike. He was a mischievous shape-shifter, using his deceptions to cause all sorts of havoc. He was always stirring up trouble with his taunts and dares."

"Were there any girl gods?" asked Anders curiously.

"Oh, yes, there were the Valkyrie, mighty warrior women led by the goddess, Freya. She rode a chariot pulled by great and large cats as *the other Valkyrie would follow her on flying horses into many battles."*

Over the course of the afternoon, Scot Mikkelson regaled Anders with many stories of gods, goddesses, giants and monsters. Feats of strength and cunning were told as fantastic creatures, horrible wolves and frightening serpents plagued the Æsir. Anders hung on every word, who asked one final question when the tales were done.

"Are the Norse gods gone forever?"

"Who's to say, my grandson? Who's to say?"

Little Anders looked out the window at the snow covered prairie and watched the wind blow white flakes in a swirling calming dance.

He wished for a life of godlike wonder and adventure.

CHAPTER FOUR

DIALOGUE WITH THE IMMORTAL SEAL

Driftwood woke up in a dazed and bewildered state. The last thing she remembered doing was trying to count the rings of Saturn. She was back looking at the snowy surface of Ellesmere Island.

"What happened?" she asked aloud to herself.

"You rose up in the air for a brief time," she was informed by a husky yet lyrical voice, "and then you were lowered down."

"That was just a brief time?" responded

Driftwood. "Felt like an eternity."

"Every individual moment is an eternity."

"Interesting idea. Can I ask you a question?"

"Of course."

"I'm talking with you?"

"Yes."

"And you're a seal?"

"A very old seal but that is not why we are talking."

"Well, why then?" inquired Driftwood.

"I believe you have been given both a great gift," explained the Immortal Seal, "and a true burden by the glorious Sedna."

"And that is?"

"You can now talk to animals and more importantly, animals can talk to you."

"Wow. I guess I owe you an apology."

"For what?"

"Trying to kill you."

"Yes, well, you certainly haven't been the first and you definitely won't be the last. I have taken advantage of Sedna's protection many times. You humans have been consistent in nothing if not your attempt to destroy me."

"I'm sorry for all that, too."

"No point being sorry for something bigger than you."

"Yes, there is."

"What do you mean, human?"

"There is a point in being sorry for things bigger than you. It is important to feel sorrow even for things that you didn't cause. It is the only way I can approach all the horribleness of the world. I use my bad feelings to try and make things better."

"Do you now?"

"Yes."

"And how was hunting me making things better?"

"That was before."

"Before what?"

"Before I saw things through universal eyes, the way that gods and godesses see."

"And how did that affect you?"

"I'm now reminded that many people and creatures need my help."

"And what do you plan to do?"

"Save the whales. Stop the giants."

"Big tasks, little one. Are you up to them?"

"Just watch me."

Chapter Five

Harry Gets Relief

"Aargh!" screamed Harry Blekansit. "I am so tired of farting. Fetch me my lunch and get that mariachi band to come play for me."

All of the servants had become quite busy tending to Harry's needs. He was very demanding for someone who hadn't left the washroom for almost four weeks. The butlers, cooks and maids were all running around fulfilling his every wish for food, medical attention, entertainment and clean underwear. They were so busy that they didn't notice a hooded woman wrapped in dark robes quietly enter through the front door.

Security had lessoned considerably since Hans had been turned into a pig and then a rabbit. There was less to protect with the theft of the baby Eaderion, the gold statues and the Galaxy Jungle 3000. However, even in perfect health, Harry had never been one for the details of business. The details he had concerned the staff with had focused entirely on his immediate needs. The best doctors in the world had not been able to cure him of his stinky affliction. Harry had resigned himself to working things through in his washroom. He consoled himself with a never-ending and never-repeating barrage of musicians.

People with horns, violins, guitars and sombreros were gathering and rehearsing in the front hall as the intruder walked stealthily and knowingly up the main stairs and made her way to Harry's wing. She walked past Harry's unused bed towards his washroom. After performing in the bathtub, the musicians

All of the servants had become quite
busy tending to Harry's needs.

of a four string quartet were packing up their instruments.

"Get out of here, you classical morons," yelled Harry. "I have more music showing up any minute."

He looked up to see the mysterious lady standing gracefully in the doorway.

"Are you one of the mariachis?" inquired Harry rudely. "Where's your instrument?"

"I am not a musician, dear," she responded as she pulled a wand out of her robes, "although you could say I am a form of conductor."

"Why are you here?" demanded Harry.

"To help you with your ailment," she said as she waved her wand. "Gas pass."

Harry could suddenly feel a peace in his stomach that he hadn't felt for quite some time. The farting had subsided. Harry stood up straight for the first time in almost a month. His knees emitted pulses of pain as their muscles expanded to positions recently ignored. Harry was undeterred by the stiffness as he enjoyed the new inner peace of his internal organs. He looked with gratitude at his cloaked benefactor.

"And to tell you," the woman continued as she pulled off her hood, "that I love you, my son."

"Mother!" exclaimed Harry who hadn't seen anything but a picture of his mother since he was four. "You've returned. And you know magic?"

"Yes, Dear. Now give me a moment to freshen up and then we'll find your father. Time to be a family again."

Chapter Six

What do Gods Know?

Silla of the Wind and Rain
Help me stop a horrible pain

Silla of the Wind and Rain
Flow against all of evil's gain

Driftwood repeated her chants over and over again. She had her eyes closed. She knew what she was waiting for. After a while the air around her began to flow at a rapid and determined pace. Driftwood could feel the currents bend around her ear. She was soon able to decipher a voice amidst the whooshes.

"*WHY HAVE YOU CONNECTED WITH ME?*" a gaseous aspect asked.

In Inuit beliefs, Silla is a deity that has no physical form. Silla is the idea that human conciousness can relate to weather through a hidden path - a path that Driftwood had discovered through powerful meditation and poetic mantras.

"*WHAT DO YOU WANT?*" the weather entity demanded.

Driftwood knew to be brief.

"Travel," she stated bluntly.

"*OH, I'VE HEARD OF YOU…*"

Rose had seen the weather change fast at Camp Magee but she had never before seen a cloud float down to the middle of the game field. She had been so taken aback by the massive mist that it took a few moments to notice her best friend sitting impossibly on top of the great fog. Things suddenly made sense.

"Only you, Drifty," commented Rose, not even seeking an explanation. "So what's up now?"

"There are whales in danger in the Norwegian Sea," explained Driftwood, "and it looks like Stormy and Tide are caught up in it. Old Bart, Murph and Grandpa Hermit are also having trouble with the giants."

"Let's ride."

"Stop laughing at me!" Thor yelled at Tide. "You should see what I can do with my hammer!"

"But I wasn't laughing," explained Tide. "In fact, I'm scared out of my mind."

After Tide's admission of fear, Thor made a strange look. He then proceeded to hug Tide with his mighty arms.

"Ha-ha-ha, your honesty is refreshing," enthused Thor. "I find mead helps to forget the frightening fates but it doesn't help with the general mockery that surrounds me."

Thor then picked a fight with the corpse that lay on the deck.

"Stop laughing at me!" the Thunder God hollered as he repeatedly punched the dead whale in the gut.

What a loonie, thought Tide, *among a flock. All of these guys are a few pancakes short of a stack.*

Tide looked over at Thor's brother who was admiring himself in the mirror.

"Who's the most beautiful of them all?" the vanity god asked, answered and responded. "You are, Balder, you most definitely are. Why, thank you."

Balder then proceeded to kiss himself in the mirror.

"I am truth. I am true. I don't lie," mumbled Tyr to himself as he walked by Tide. "I am truth. I am true. I don't lie."

Tyr shook his right arm towards the ocean. Missing from it was his hand.

"And here is the truest statement from

Tyr," the old god yelled. "I shall have victory over all monsters and particular revenge over the great wolf, Fenrir, for his brutal taking of my hand."

Suddenly a god with fiery orange hair and much more diminutive stature than the others came and tapped Tyr on the shoulder.

"Look over there," pointed Loki, "it's the Midgard Serpent."

"Where?" cried Tyr, turning around to look in the direction that Loki had indicated feverishly ready for battle.

"I mean over there," Loki corrected himself. "Isn't that Garm the Hound?"

"End of days!" cried a panicky Tyr. "Why can't I see these doom bringers?"

"Ooops," blurted the trickster god, "but I think over the horizon is Hel, queen of Niflheim, the cowards' underworld."

"Eeeeiii!" screamed the war god as he waved his battleaxe needlessly into the air.

"Tee-hee," giggled Loki.

At the bow of the boat, where the giant

harpoon was mounted, stood Stormy and the captain. The captain watched over the others as he scratched underneath the patch of his missing eye.

"What a crew," sighed Odin. "I often think it has been a miracle that we have survived at all in the new world."

"You are gods after all," observed Stormy.

"Small advantage in these modern times," commented the father god as he petted the barrel of the harpoon gun. "Even us immortals have to rely on technology to survive. That is where your accurate shooting has come in handy."

A tear suddenly welled up in Odin's one good eye. He placed his forehead against the gun and began to bawl uncontrollably.

"I gave a pupil to Mimir to become all knowing," explained Odin with sorrow. "Now I understand the ways of the world but I have no depth perception. I couldn't hit the broad side of a castle. 'Twas a horrible tragedy until I discovered your fair aim, Stormy. We shall thrive once again and be awash in whale blubber due to you, young lad."

"Yeah, it's really," Stormy paused briefly before finishing his sentence, "great. Really, really great."

What a loonie, thought Stormy. *What have I gotten us into?*

As Stormy lamented his situation he looked out to the great big sea. He hoped that no one would spot another whale. He was still feeling nauseous from slaying the first one. Fortunately, all he could see were emerald waves and clear sky. Except in the distance there was a distinctly isolated cloud. He stared pensively at the billowy fluff until he was interrupted by the maniacal screaming of Tyr.

"I see one!" Tyr cried as he waved his handless right arm towards the tail fin of a nearby whale that could be seen arching into and out of the water. "By the spouts, you shall not escape me."

"All hands on deck," ordered Odin. "Thor,

steer us towards the beast ."

"With pleasure, father," responded Thor manning the helm, "as I'm sure I heard this whale laughing at me."

Balder was still making out with himself. Loki was now standing beside Odin. Stormy was at the turret of the harpoon. Tide looked frustratingly on as they neared their quarry. He decided to do something to quell his discomfort.

"Captain Odin, please reconsider," Tide requested. "After centuries of being hunted, these whales are quite endangered. Your actions bring nothing new to this era. Only more anguish and pain."

Odin began to weep.

"Perhaps you are right, mortal," the All-Father confided. "This feels like a horrible way to enter the new eon."

"Now, now, Odin," interrupted Loki. "Remember that whales are bigger than you."

"This is true," confirmed Odin.

"Perhaps you are right, mortal," the All-Father confided. "This feels like a horrible way to enter the new eon."

"And all things bigger must be battled. That is a warrior's way."

"Thank you for your reassuringly old logic, Loki," stated Odin as he looked out at the whale that appeared ever closer, "and now you shall fire at will, Stormy."

The whale continued to swim the surface, unaware of the steady site that was now aimed at her. She couldn't hear Stormy whisper a sincere apology to her. She was totally oblivious to the squeezing of the trigger. The powder that exploded created a tiny boom that she could register. This sound did not help her know about the harpoon that was heading towards her heart. She was ignorant of her impending doom.

The harpoon left the barrel with scientific accuracy. The missile cut through the air and flew unerringly towards its prey. Having no ears the spear could not hear what was about to be said.

"Hey bah la ba hoo ba lee bay kow kow kow," sang Driftwood to the background of

Rose snapping as the two sat a top a cloud. "Kree bop a loop a bay way now dow lao."

The whale felt a slight tingle as a giant dandelion struck its side. She did not know that mere moments earlier the flower had been a fatal projectile transformed from the skat magic of a young girl.

"That tickled," observed the whale.

"Are you alright?" asked Driftwood.

"You are the first human who has ever asked me that. I am fine, sweet one, although I seem to have lost some of my colleagues."

"It may be too late for them," lamented Driftwood, "but I shall do my best to save you and your other friends."

"Fare thee well, dear child."

CHAPTER SEVEN

A SHORT TALE OF BREAK UP AND THEFT

For four years, Hans and Helena had been happy together in their marriage. They had met on the TV game show, Fight for Love, where Helena had won a series of competitions in which first prize was to become the wife of Hans Blekansit. The couple had started a life on Grand Cayman Island where Hans built a beautiful manor and Helena gave birth to Harry Blekansit.

Helena had raised Harry while Hans tended to the infant Eaderion in the backyard of their *mansion. The mystical creature received more attention from Hans than Harry received from his own father. Harry would torture the baby beast in hopes of gaining the approval of Hans. Strangely enough, it worked.*

"Making the Eaderion hate us improves her ability to invent things that humans will want," he would explain to his son when Helena wasn't around. "The hate makes her create brilliant psychological traps that everyone must buy. Punishing her is a key to our power. Well done."

Helena slowly began to wonder why her son was becoming so mean. Harry spent all his time coming up with ways to hurt the Eaderion. Helena hoped it was just the misplaced energy of a three-year-old.

Hans would return from New York, anxious about the adult Eaderion's low productivity. In Great Blekansit Tower on Wall Street, Hans kept a second older Eaderion connected to the world via its cobweb of silk and wire. This creature would spin up games and distractions that people would consume in massive quantities. It had made Heinz Blekansit a rich man before his disappearance and supposed death. Hans had followed in his father's footsteps but was struggling to maintain his father's empire. He had never been taught any magic so he was basically following his instincts, forever feeling anger towards his father. He hated his father for never teaching him anything. It was wrath and greed that had inspired Hans to blow up his parent's airplane before they could follow through with their intention of giving the family money away.

Hans had hidden much of his anger from Helena. On a stormy night he finally revealed his darker side.

Helena was changing Harry's diaper when Hans came home after a rough day in New York.

"How was work, Honey?" asked Helena.

"Work," retorted Hans. "What would you know about work?"

"Pardon me?"

"Everyday, I have to go to Wall Street and deal with problems that you can't even imagine. All you have to do is enjoy the fruits of my labour."

"Have you said hello to Harry yet?"

"Don't change the subject. Have you gained weight?"

After four years, Hans and Helena were not happy together in their marriage.

Their fights intensified for months, occurring with more and more frequency amidst long terms of silence. Eventually an argument ended with Hans striking Helena.

The next day Helena packed a few things as she prepared to flee from Blekansit Manor. She wanted to take Harry with her but had no money of her own. She knew he would be fed and clothed at his father's and she couldn't make that same guarantee. Before she was finished she went up to the attic. From underneath an old chest she pulled out a well-worn leather-bound book. On the front read The Magic of Heinz Blekansit.

"Stealing this will make things right," Helena whispered to herself.

CHAPTER EIGHT

A FLICK OF THE WRIST

"Thwarted," exclaimed Odin, "by some girls! Stop them, Gods!"

The first to act was Tyr who had been on the edge of fury for quite some time. The arrival of Driftwood and Rose on their cloud was all it took to tip him over. In mere moments he had climbed the crow's nest and had lunged himself toward the young ladies, axe in hand.

"Eeeeiiiiii-yi-yi-yi!" Tyr emitted as his battle cry.

"Plan yet?" inquired Rose.

"On it," assured Driftwood as she reached into her bag of runes. She quickly pulled out a stone with an arrow-like symbol.

She held the rune directly towards the fast approaching god, pointing the symbol's face at him. She then proceeded to do two things.

First, she started with a chant.

Tiewaz of the warlord's firm ground
Flip his silly-willy machismo around

Second, she twisted her wrist causing the pointed top of the symbol to be directed downwards.

"Eeeeiiiiii-yi-yi," continued Tyr. "Yi-yi-why? Why? Why?"

With his two arms he carefully clutched the double blade of his axe into his chest. By the time he gently landed on the pillowy cloud he had curled himself into a ball. He writhed about like a disoriented infant.

"The blade cuts and kills yet solves not my woes," Tyr contemplated as he slowly stood up, regaining his composure and holding the axe with his one good hand. "I am done with you."

Tyr tossed his age-old weapon into the sea. He then stared gracefully at the whale to which he had previously expressed such unprovoked rage.

"Ah, massive and peaceful beast," he serenaded, "I will now protect you with my love."

The war god jumped off the thick fog and landed on the back of the whale. With both arms and legs he hugged her tail fin with all his might.

"More affection," the whale could be

heard saying nearby Driftwood, "from a second person in one day. How bizarre."

"If any go for you they will have to get through me," expressed Tyr, waving his handless arm in the air.

"Nice," commented Rose.

Odin had been watching the whole incident from the Asgard's bow.

"You are quite the power player, meddling with the motives of the ancients," observed Odin. "Especially those of Tyr the True."

"I just redirected his energy," explained Driftwood, "and possibly introduced him to deeper truths. Really, he got there himself by merely questioning a little. Asking *Why?* can be very profound."

"Something I've been doing much of as of late," confessed the All-Father. "It has been difficult for me to feel comfortable since being summoned into what you call the 21st century. Hunting and killing do not feel glorious in this era and my sons and colleagues have more problems than I realized."

"Summoned?" repeated Driftwood as she and Rose stepped on the deck of the boat. "Who summoned you?"

"Uh, that would be me," confessed Stormy. "Hey, Rose. Hi ya, Drifty. Nice to see you."

The three friends hugged.

"Where's Tide?" Driftwood adamantly asked.

"Over here," said Tide as he stood beside the ship's mast. "I've just been trying to steer clear of the chaos."

Loki suddenly ran past Tide with Thor chasing and yelling, "Stop laughing at me!"

Meanwhile, Balder was still kissing himself in the mirror.

"You're the cutest. No, you are," he gushed to himself. "No, you are. No, you are. OK, on the count of three let's both say *you are*. One…Two…"

"They're all mad here," stated Tide. "All because Stormy wanted to be like you."

"Wanted to be like me?" asked Driftwood.

She was hurt that Tide was so bluntly condemning and determined not to let Tide know that she was offended. "What do I have to do with this?"

"I kept hearing from Rose how you were summoning gods and doing all sorts of amazing things," explained Stormy. "When I was in the woods of the Lofoten Islands in northern Norway I discovered an ancient viking household. It looked like it had been abandoned for centuries. Inside was a small chest containing tiny figures carved of wood and bone. They looked like old children's toys but I recognized them immediately as icons of Odin, Thor, Balder, Tyr and Loki – Norse Gods of olden times. Without really knowing what I was doing, I placed the dolls in a pentagram around me and began what became a lengthy and improvised ritual that combined meditation and chanting. Eventually, this great ship arose from the ocean. It was fun at first, spending time with powerful gods. So much fun that I sent for

Tide. However, by the time he got here I realized that I had made a horrible mistake. I had no way to control them. Their passionate thrill for blood became too much to oppose. I got caught up in it and have done regrettable things."

Stormy began to weep.

Rose comforted him.

"Don't beat yourself up about it," she advised. "You've got to remember that Driftwood has had years of training. Playing with magic carelessly can lead to one mess out of Ma-Joley."

"Do you practice magic, Rose?" Stormy asked.

"I prefer to leave that job to Driftwood. I strive to bring the moxy."

"What am I going to do if I shouldn't summon gods and cast spells?"

"I don't know, Storm-boy. Model trains?"

"I need to rest," admitted Stormy. "I'm going to go to my mother's home in Strongfield."

"Rose is right. Magic is very dangerous," cautioned Driftwood as a twinkle came to her eye. "However, I think we can take advantage of your efforts."

Driftwood started to walk. Tide joined her.

"Hey, Driftwood, I'm sorry that I was so harsh before."

"You couldn't have said hello?"

"I haven't slept well recently but I know that's no excuse. Anyways, it's nice to see you, Witchy."

Driftwood normally didn't like being given names but she enjoyed Tide's playful teasing.

"A fine mess you got yourself into, Tidy," she quipped. "I can't jump on clouds everyday and fly around the world to save you."

"Drifty, you fly around the world almost every week. This was going to be my big traveling adventure but I spent all my money getting here. The Asgard have yet to pay me so I had to stay working for them or I'd starve to death. I need to get to Camp Magee to make some money."

"Don't worry, Tide. We'll get you there. I have a plan that I think will really turn all this horrible mess around."

Driftwood walked up to the one-eyed lord god.

"Odin," she brazenly called out.

"What is it, child?" cried the deflated leader. "Haven't you done enough?"

"Do you like fighting giants?"

Chapter Nine

In a Back Alley

Hans nibbled on a Styrofoam cup hoping to get sustenance from the residue of the coffee stained inside. The caffeine was making his little rabbit heart beat even faster. He did not even notice when two people walked up to the dumpster behind Great Blekansit Tower where he had found refuge since being changed into a hare by Driftwood. His eyes darted past their ankles without registering. Even if he could see them he wouldn't have noticed one of them waving her arms. However, he could hear when she spoke.

"Change be gone," she chanted.

Hans grew back to being human.

"Revenge," was his first word followed by, "daughter."

"Hello, father," greeted Harry.

"Revenge...daughter."

Hans looked up to see his son and a woman he recognized immediately.

"Helena?" he inquired. "Is that you?"

"How have you been, Hans?" Helena asked.

"I've been a rabbit," Hans bluntly returned, ignoring Harry as he questioned his ex-wife. "Did you change me back? How did you learn magic?"

"You really never explored your attic much did you, dear?" Helena responded. "I found something up there that you would have loved."

"And what was that?"

"Your father's magic book."

"Really?"

*"Revenge," was his first word
followed by, "daughter."*

"Yes."

"So you've learnt his magic?"

"Yes."

"And now you're back?"

"Yes."

"Why?"

"To be a family again."

"Do you still love me, Helena?"

"Of course not, Hans. You're much too ruthless."

"Then why are you back?"

"Well, so that Harry could be with his mother again. Or had you forgotten that he is my son?"

"How could I forget with his behaviour? What else do you want?"

"Why, your money, of course. Combined with my magic, darling, we can't lose."

Chapter Ten

Nothing Better Than a Good Compromise

"Wake up, friend," urged Murph Magee as he shook Old Bart by the shoulder. "He's about to vomit."

"Whub habbened?" asked Old Bart as he opened his eyes.

"We stopped one giant," explained Hermit the Laughing Man, "but there was a second one. I think he broke my arm."

"As well as my leg," added Murph.

"By bose," sputtered Bart as he put his

hands over his face. "I cab bareby sbeak."

"So much for our triumphant reunion," complained Murph. "We stopped only one giant before getting put out of commission."

"Better than none," joked Hermit. "Although we haven't even saved St. John's from getting a dreaded Blekan-Mart."

"Book ub dare," stumbled Old Bart. "He's starbing."

As Andrews the Giant had put his hands on his knees, he started to cough and hack over Signal Hill, on the coast of the small Newfoundland city.

The three men looked up with remorse. They were anticipating the huge mega-store that was about to emerge from the innards of the near mindless goliath.

"Consume…aack…produce," belched Andrews, "consume…urgh…produce."

The corner of the store began to appear out of Andrews' mouth. Just as the *t* in the Blekan-Mart sign became visible did the giant hear the voice of someone from the nearby ocean.

"Is that laughter coming out of your mouth?" asked Thor as he flew through the air.

The thunder god had just jumped from the deck of the Asgard, now located in St. John's harbour. Driftwood had told him that the giant's gagging sounds translated into laughter and Thor was quick to believe it was directed at him. As he approached the corporate colossus, he swung his hammer around and around preparing to strike.

"Let's see you laugh after feeling the sting of Mjöllnir the Destroyer," roared Thor as he vigorously struck the store with his hammer.

It was an effective blow. The store flew back down Andrews' throat and didn't stop until it landed in the pit of his stomach. The giant had become winded from having the Blekan-Mart rammed back into his bellows. He began to wheeze which Thor predictably misinterpreted.

"More mockery!" cried Thor as he jumped

off the top of Signal Hill.

Mjöllnir the Hammer connected perfectly with Andrews' chin. The impact caused the giant to fly into the air. He sailed for a great distance before landing in the middle of the Atlantic Ocean.

"Now that was a battle most glorious," commented Odin as he watched from the Asgard. "You say there are more of these monstrosities?"

"Thanks to my nasty father," explained Driftwood, "they are all over North America. Puking up community-wrecking stores wherever they may go."

"This is a quest that I can lead us on," stated Odin dramatically. "Tyr has decided to protect whales so I shall take Thor, Loki and Balder with me on a journey to stop these giants. Perhaps there is still some use in us old gods."

"Fare thee well, Odin," said Driftwood. "It's nice of you to help the world."

Driftwood caught up to Rose who had

already left the ship to reunite with the three injured wizards.

Rose was helping Murph stand up when Driftwood ran up and hugged Bart and Hermit.

"Old Bart! Grandpa!" exclaimed Driftwood. "Are you alright?"

"I bwoke by bose," informed Old Bart.

"Pardon me?" responded Driftwood.

"He broke his nose," clarified Hermit, "and I, my arm."

"We sure took a beating," lamented a limping Murph.

"Hey, you did your best," comforted Rose. "According to Swamp, that's all any of us can do."

"Thank you, Rose," returned Murph as he gave her a big hug. "I should listen to my grandson more. I forget what a positive influence he's been on all of you camp counselors."

"Cut," a voice interrupted, "and that's a wrap for now, Ernie. Go take a break."

A woman in a bright red business suit was suddenly walking towards them while a large hairy man had lowered a camera and was walking away. Before anyone knew it, the woman was shaking hands with Driftwood.

"Hello there, Driftwood Ellesmere, it is a sincere pleasure," the woman stated. "I have been following your image for quite some time."

"Image?" Driftwood responded.

"Oh, yes, you photograph very well. The footage I've amassed is truly impressive."

"Footage?"

"Oh, yes. You would be amazed at where cameras are these days. Everything is being digitally chronicled. It's just a matter of finding quality content. And you, my dear, are building a fantastic portfolio."

"Content? Portfolio?"

"I can see it now," spoke the woman as she pulled out a small video player from her pocket. "Watch Driftwood Ellesmere and her invisible friend Rose fight a spidery, liony, birdy thing."

The small video player was showing footage of when Driftwood and Rose fought the adult Eaderion.

"This is from a security tape retrieved from Great Blekansit Towers," explained the woman, "and we got this one from the personal video camera of a recently thwarted African slave driver."

The video player showed Driftwood and Rose as they freed the trapped children of a chocolate slave farm. Everyone watched as the children's chains became flimsy string and the slave masters were wrapped in dirt moving from Driftwood's magic.

"Holy Ma-Joley," chimed in Rose, "I never knew we were being recorded."

"That's what makes the footage so natural," continued the woman, "and I have more. A hiker got you fighting a giant in Squamish on his cell phone camera. Some environmentalists just filmed you saving a whale. We even have you failing to free the children of a toy factory in Shanghai. Don't worry. I'm pretty sure I can spin that falter into some serious character development. Not always succeeding adds a bit of drama to it all."

"Who awe boo?" demanded Old Bart.

"I believe what my friend is trying to say," Murph interpreted, "is who are you?"

"My name is Betty Hays," introduced the woman. "I own Hays Quantum Communications, also known as HQC, and I come here with a wonderful opportunity for Driftwood."

"What is it?" inquired Driftwood.

"Do you want to be a star?"

CHAPTER ELEVEN

MEDIA GRAVITATION

"No, I don't," responded Driftwood.

"Did you here what I said?" asked Betty. "No one ever says 'no' to that question."

"You show images of me on TV and say you want to make me a star. Well, I don't like TV. TV tries to sell people needless things. People superficially go on it hoping for things like love when all they get is deception."

"Didn't your parents meet on a TV show?"

"Don't remind me. My father met all

his wives on some stupid show called *Fight for Love.* He's a rich man with a horrible personality."

"You're an angry girl, Driftwood. The audience will really connect with that but it probably won't test well if you overdo it."

"Stop talking like that!"

"Like what?"

"Like I have an audience."

"Everyone has an audience, sweetheart. All the world's a stage and all that. Hays Quantum Communications would just give you a bigger soapbox to stand on. We'll really get you out there. Think of all the good you could do."

"What do you mean?"

"Aren't you trying to save the world?"

"I guess so."

"Well, if you let me turn you into a celebrity, many more people could hear your message. You could change the world with clever marketing."

"Do you really think I can save the

world?"

"Just let me help you."

"Bah," snorted Hermit, "this smells of money and I don't like it."

Hermit hadn't touched money in over thirty years since his son, Hans, had killed his wife, Stephanie Blekansit, over their family fortune.

"There is something familiarly suspicious about this," added Murph. "I agree with your grandfather."

"Bee boo," affirmed Old Bart.

"You really should be careful, Drifty," warned Rose. "This seems like a weird deal."

"If you meet with me in New York I can show you my first proposal," invited Betty, "which is to create Driftwood and Rose action figures."

"But maybe we should hear what she has to say," reversed Rose as she imagined dolls of herself being on the shelves of toy stores everywhere. "So, Betty, do you have a jet?"

Chapter Twelve

Broken Conversations

Rose and Driftwood were soon sitting next to each other on a private jet. They were flying over Broadview, Saskatchewan when Driftwood broke what had been a lengthy awkward pause in conversation that had existed since before they took off.

"Wow."

"Agreed."

"Did we just do that?"

"Do what?" responded Rose. "Go to New York City and sign our images over to a giant media company? Yes, I believe we did."

"Did we do the right thing?" contemplated Driftwood.

"It's like Betty said. This way we can get our message out to more people."

"Rose?"

"Yeah, Drifty?"

"Do you remember if we ever actually explained our message to Betty?"

"Uh…"

"I don't think we did. In fact, do you even know what our message is? I'd never thought about it before Betty told us we had one."

"Uh…"

The two girls began another long, uncomfortable and slightly guilt-ridden session of not talking. Hays Quantum Communications had given them a free trip on their company jet back to Vancouver, the city closest to Camp Magee, and neither of the girls were enjoying it.

Driftwood was still surprised at herself, at how easily she had signed over her image to a company. The experience of seeing herself on the video screen had caused an unexpected growing of her self-esteem that had clouded her judgment. Not speaking to Rose, Driftwood had time to remember when she was eleven and some documentary film-makers were staying at the Toque and Mitt Inn while shooting a show about Arctic Wolves. The film crew followed the wolves everywhere, capturing every moment of the graceful creatures of the north. Driftwood, who was initially enamoured by the glamour of the documentary production, watched as the cameraman crawled into a cave where a mother had left a litter of pups while she went out searching for food. Driftwood imagined all the excellent footage that the man was capturing of cute little wolves crawling about. The crew returned to the Toque and Mitt. Driftwood followed quickly as any youthful onlooker tends to when watching the labours of admirable adults. Unbeknownst to the crew or Driftwood, when the mother wolf returned she could smell that a human had been in her home and, fearing for her safety, she ran off and left her children behind. Six days later, while on a playful hike, Driftwood discovered the corpses of the wee babies, left to starve to death. Since then, she often reflected on how people seldom think about the unknown negative impacts that filmmaking can produce. The camera, itself, is a potentially dangerous thing, and it had intoxicated Driftwood and Rose to commit to something with unknown consequences.

Rose decided to take advantage of the jet's telephone and phone Camp Magee to check in. She was quite excited when the other end picked up.

"Hey, it's Rose. Some crazy dealings happened in New York and now we're flying back to camp in a corporate jet and we're really not sure if we did the right thing and there've been more giants and also gods and whales…and…and…who is this?" Rose finally breathed in. "Oh, it's you. Yeah, she's here."

Rose silently handed the phone over without revealing who had answered.

"Hello," spoke Driftwood quietly.

"Hey, Drifter," came a familiar voice from the other end. "How's our poor little witch girl doing?"

"Fine, Tidy, thanks for asking. I guess you made it back to camp from Norway."

"Yeah, Swamp helped me fly back to Canada. It's fun to play with the kids again and be around everyone."

"I'll bet."

"We sure miss you guys."

Driftwood liked hearing that and even found the way Tide used "we" instead of "I" kind of cute in an evasive way. The two shared a silence that caused Driftwood's heart to beat faster and her throat to tighten. The quiet was intensely beautiful but also quite nerve-wracking. Driftwood wanted to say something meaningful. However, she also wanted to appear non-committal in the courting melee that may or may not have been going on. Words were forming and being dismissed in her head at an overwhelming rate.

"Soooooooooo," she finally said taking up seven entire seconds with just one syllable. Her single word was followed by another suspenseful moment. Driftwood wished she spoke like a jazz song. She finally decided to initiate a brave response.

"There's something I've wanted to say," Driftwood cautiously confessed. "I've been-"

Before Driftwood could finish, she could suddenly hear nothing but static on the other end of the phone.

"Tide? Are you there?" No response. "Tide? Tide? Tide?"

The phone had cut out. Driftwood didn't know if it had been disconnected purposefully or by accident. She didn't care.

She just hoped that Tide wasn't thinking that she had hung up on him.

Chapter Thirteen

Media Aggravation

"Something's up."

"What do you mean?"

"I was just talking to Tide and then the line went fuzzy."

"There's probably just interference in the atmosphere, Driftwood."

"I don't think so."

"Relax. You'll get to talk to your boyfriend as soon as we get back to camp."

"He's not my boyfriend, Rose."

"Relax."

The silence between the two girls restarted.

Rose looked out the window. Driftwood studied the letters HQC that were strewn all over the cabin of the plane. Letting the sound and order of the letters flow and reform in her mind she went up to the bar and poured herself an apple juice with ice and a slice of lemon.

Rose was barely paying attention when Driftwood was at the cabin bar. For a moment she thought she heard Driftwood whispering to herself but was too distracted about her conflicted feelings to concern herself with it. She was excited that a toy was going to be made after her but was nervous about not having any control over how it was to be executed by HQC.

The "lack of message" thing nagged at both of the girls.

Rose stared blankly at her sandals while Driftwood intently studied the ice in her apple juice. The tension was gratefully interrupted by a video screen that suddenly turned on.

"Hello, girls," Betty Hayes greeted. "I

hope you're enjoying your flight home."

"Actually," confessed Driftwood, "I think we want to talk to you about our message."

"No time for such details, darling," stated Betty. "I wanted to show you the commercial we've come up with."

"Commercial?" Rose expressed with shock. "We just finished our meeting with you a couple hours ago."

"Things move fast at HQC," explained Betty. "I hope you enjoy."

Suddenly the television screen was full of a sea of mesmerizing animated stars. They faded like fireworks to reveal a young boy and girl having fun playing with a couple of action figures.

One doll resembled Driftwood except the doll looked angrier and with more muscles. When the boy pushed a button on the back of the Driftwood figure the doll's leg moved in a powerful kicking motion while it screamed.

"Hii-Ya!" yelled the doll.

"I've never kicked anyone in my life,"

observed Driftwood.

When the camera did a closeup of the other doll it clearly had on Rose's clothes and hairstyle. However, the doll's face appeared to be wearing makeup and her figure was vastly disproportionate to the real Rose. The Rose doll had curvy hips, very large breasts and a waist as thin as a straw. No human had ever looked like this doll. The young girl was combing the toy Rose's silky dreadlocks and hairweaves.

"You can't comb hair like mine," commented Rose as she stroked her knots. "That's how it gets so clumpy."

"Do you like how I look?" the Rose doll asked when a button was pushed on its back. "It's the most important thing."

"I've definitely never said that," expressed Rose, "and I think that doll's bust is defying the laws of gravity."

Before the girls could say anything else, annoying music began to scream from the screen. A chorus of voices started to sing a song:

Hey Hoo There Girls
Howdy Wow Boys
Put away all
Your other toys

We've got the cure
For your boredom woes
Play with Driftwood
And her best friend Rose

With her mighty
Super Ninja-Kick
Driftwood Ellesmere
Is truly sick

With her wicked
Awesome fashion
Rose and her clothes
Will fire your passion

The commercial ended with another

cascade of exploding stars.

"Well, what do you think?" asked Betty from the screen.

"Fashion and passion? How I look is the most important thing?" Rose angrily exclaimed. "I wear ripped blue jeans and wornout plaid shirts so that I don't need to think about fashion. I could care less how I look."

"Ninja-Kick? Truly sick?" repeated Driftwood.

"All the kids say *sick* these days," advised Betty.

"I know," Driftwood dryly responded. "I'm a camp counselor."

"We tried to come up with a way that your toy could do magic," Betty further explained, "but we couldn't find a way to do the mechanics. For the Ninja-Kick all we needed was a tiny metal spring."

"What about my doll?" queried Rose. "What thinking or lack thereof inspired those mechanics?"

"We needed to further magnify your appeal," justified Betty. "Increasing certain body part sizes, making you up a bit and putting an emphasis on your outfits should increase your purchasing potential significantly."

"Yippee," Rose responded sarcastically.

"You've manipulated our images," accused Driftwood. "How is any of this saving the world?"

"It's just business, Baby," explained Betty. "I thought you'd be excited. In fact, I just sent the first trial crate of dolls to the next group of school kids who are going to your camp. I thought the campers would have fun playing with you as a toy."

"But Camp Magee is about learning and having fun in the outdoors," countered Driftwood, "not playing with plastic toys."

"But we want you to be everywhere, Starlight."

"That doll is not me! And stop with all the cutesy names! I want you to end the production of our figures immediately."

"Oh, it's too late for that. Papers have been signed. Wheels are in motion. The big company wouldn't like that."

"What big company?"

"Hays Quantum Communications is a subsidiary of a much larger corporation. Perhaps it's time to tell you that my full name," revealed the woman, "is Helena Betty Hays Blekansit."

"What?" Rose and Driftwood simultaneously cried out.

Suddenly joining Helena on the screen were Hans and Harry.

"Hello there, Daughter," greeted a stern Hans. "On behalf of Great Blekansit Products I want to thank you for making us a bit wealthier and then I just have one more thing to say to you."

The two young girls responded with completely stunned silence as the air around them started to rush around. They were too distracted to notice both the pilot and flight attendant clad in parachutes and jumping out the airplane door.

"Revenge," concluded Hans immediately before the plane proceeded to explode.

Chapter Fourteen

Tension in the Tower

The video screen that Hans was staring at suddenly went from showing his daughter holding a glass of juice to displaying snowy static.

"Excellent," said Hans. "The bomb worked. Now, I'll never be thwarted by my daughter again."

"And just before she died she gave us permission to use her image for anything," added Helena. "We'll get rich off of her past heroics."

"Perfect," Hans joyously remarked.

"Is there anything I can do to help?" inquired Harry.

"All the work is already being done, Harry," explained Helena. "Just sit back and reap the benefits of your parents' successful efforts. Meanwhile, your father and I have to review the operations in China. You can come along if you want."

Helena and Hans hurried off to the top floor of the tower. Since the first giant had grown through the roof, the grand hall was also acting as the new helicopter launch pad. Harry followed his parents as they continued to generally ignore him. Although he was twenty-one, Harry tended to think more like a twelve-year-old. Since the baby Eaderion had been stolen he had nothing to torture. This was what he had previously done to get the attention of his father. Without the infant creature to throw things at, Harry felt like he had no way to get Hans' approval.

As the family climbed the stairs to the

rooftop, the son fixated on each changing step in front of his face.

More than one step, Harry thought, *is just like more than one way to look at life.*

Hans interrupted Harry's first philosophical moment by barking at him from the helicopter.

"Quit staring at the stairway and hurry up!" his father yelled over the roar of the propellers.

Harry made his way to his seat, disaffected by Hans' bellowing and brawling.

Maybe getting my parent's acceptance isn't worth worrying about, contemplated Harry. *Could there be more important things?*

CHAPTER FIFTEEN

THE AIR UP THERE

Rose watched as flames suddenly engulfed the video screen that she had been staring at. The fire looked to expand and radiate in every direction. However, before it could break through the hull of the plane or even reached the girl's seats, it seemed to move as if controlled by an outside force. All of the heat and flame seemed to funnel towards Driftwood's glass, except it wasn't a glass at all. For the first time, Rose noticed that Driftwood had put the apple juice into her

Mason jar.

That must be some potion, thought Rose.

Glowing smoke condensed and entered the top of the jar. Rose could hear Driftwood repeat a chant over and over:

Oh clear ice cube
Tiny chilly orb
Take this thermal energy
And please do absorb

The light show soon ended as the last of the explosion entered the jar. Driftwood put her hand inside and pulled out an ice cube that appeared to be shining intensely from its centre.

"I have to throw this out of the plane," explained Driftwood as she unbuckled her seat belt, "before the cube releases all of its stored energy!"

"Don't let go of my hand!" screamed Rose over the vacuum.

The pilot and flight attendant had left the

door open when they jumped out. Air had been leaving the cabin rapidly. Driftwood stretched her body to the door reaching for the entryway with one hand. She threw the ice cube out and then quickly shut the door. Just as she secured the hatch did a bright light flash through the window. The ice cube had exploded out of distance of the plane which, as it had no pilot, was rushing towards the ground.

"Holy Ma-Joley!" yelled Rose. "Do you have a plan for this?"

"I could turn our bodies into rubber," contemplated the young mage. "We might survive if the plane only crashes and doesn't explode."

"Anything else?" inquired Rose as she desperately lunged for the cockpit. "Maybe I can figure out how to fly this thing."

The cockpit door was locked.

"Well, that's just dandy!" cried Rose.

Driftwood was having a hard time coming up with a plan. It had taken a lot of thinking to realize that the letters that came before HQC were G,P and B. Rearrange them and you get GBP or Great Blekansit Products. Once she had made the possible connection and knowing her father's propensity towards blowing up planes, Driftwood had prepared a suitable potion to deal with a bomb. She hadn't thought of what to do after that. She was also dealing with the uncontrollable jealousy that she felt when she saw Harry, her half-brother, with his mother. It reminded her that her own mother was dead. Her frustrated emotions distracted her from the crisis at hand. She had become very good at thinking in stressful situations but she was drawing a blank on any life saving ideas.

"Maybe there are more parachutes," Rose frantically said as she ripped open every cupboard in the cabin.

A barrage of serving trays, oxygen masks and life jackets came flying out during her search. She suddenly studied a small bundle with interest.

"This will have to do," she exclaimed as she put the parcel under her arm.

Rose grabbed Driftwood and went over to the door. She took off her belt and tied it to some handles that were on the outside of the wrapped plastic. She pulled the emergency release lever of the plane and the cabin door flew off. She then held tight onto a cord attached to the bundle.

"Hold on tight, Drifty," Rose commanded as the two girls jumped out of the plane.

Rose pulled the cord and the package started to fill up with air. Her belt had been strapped onto two sides of an expanding emergency raft. As the boat took on its upside-down form, it filled up with a pillowing pocket of air creating a makeshift parachute. Rose held onto the belt with her hands and secured Driftwood with her legs. The two girls watched as the plane fell far below them and crashed onto a farmer's field.

"That was close."

"Good work, Rose," acknowledged Driftwood, "I got lost in my own thoughts for a second but I'm OK now. Thank you."

"Don't thank me just yet," commented Rose. "We're still falling pretty fast. We could really use an updraft."

"I'll see what I can do," said Driftwood as she closed her eyes and tried to meditate while plummeting to the ground.

"I thought you said you wouldn't get lost in your own thoughts again," observed Rose, "because I could really use a hand here."

Suddenly a surging gust blew in and went up into the raft. Instead of falling downwards the girls started to float sideways. The raft had become a glider. Rose could hear a voice emit from the air that was rushing past and bouncing inside her ears.

"*I HAVE NO HANDS*," Silla the weather entity replied, "*BUT WILL A WELL DIRECTED WIND DO?*"

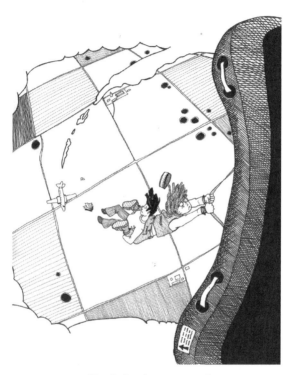

"Don't thank me just yet."

Chapter Sixteen

Negative Influences

By the time Rose and Driftwood were gliding over the border between Alberta and British Columbia they were sitting on the belt that held the raft in an arcing shape. The strap had become an uncomfortable perch as they glided for hours with the aid of Silla's control of the currents. After hours of travel via the upside-down raft, they finally reached Camp Magee in the Elaho Valley near Squamish.

Thank you, Silla, Driftwood said inside her head.

"*FLOAT THEE WELL, BRAVE DRIFT-WOOD,*" Silla blew ominously, "*FOR YOUR CHALLENGES ARE JUST BEGINNING.*"

With a quick gale Silla caused the rubber raft to flip over. The girls were sitting chaotically with limbs flailing everywhere as the boat was lowered beside the front entrance of the camp. Rose and Driftwood helped each other stand up.

"I wish I could say it was my arms that were tired after that trip," quipped Rose, "but it's my rear-end that's really sore. Why didn't Silla just carry us on a cloud like before?"

"I guess gods can be kind of unpredictable," contemplated Driftwood before they were interrupted by the approaching sounds of engines and tires.

"That must be the next group of campers," ventured Rose as the rumbles got louder.

Instead of seeing the expected yellow school bus drive from over the hill, there were two vans each with their own satellite dishes and numerous other automobiles all trying to outrace each other. The vehicles all skidded to stops as people armed with microphones, notepads and laptops rushed out and ran frantically towards the girls. Driftwood was instantly inundated with a barrage of questions from the stampede of journalists.

"Are you the Driftwood Ellesmere that the newest action figure, due to be released by HQC and GBP, is modeled after?

"What's it like to be a toy?"

"Are you really the daughter of two-time *Fight for Love* star Hans Blekansit? Was it this relationship that led to you being merchandised?"

"What happened to your mother?"

"Where were you raised?"

Some of the press turned their attention to Rose. The media had an unnerving amount of prior personal knowledge and a needless desire to learn the most trivial pieces of information.

"Were you really a homeless street girl before ending up at Camp Magee?"

"What's it like being Driftwood's side-kick?"

"How did you get your hair to look like that?"

"Where do you buy your clothes?"

"Hair? Clothes? Sidekick?" responded Rose. "You sure are interested in the important stuff. And I'm more like a smarty-pants partner."

Driftwood was starting to feel nauseous. The crowd of reporters had made her feel like she was in a busy airport or bus station. She always found those areas far too overwhelming with people. Her years of being raised in quiet surroundings always became apparent in these situations, as was her usual response. She shut her eyes, sat on the ground and began to do her breathing in hopes of calming herself down.

"Are you casting a spell?" inquired one reporter.

"Or summoning a god?" suggested another.

"If you know so much about magic," asked a third, "why haven't you saved the world yet?"

The last question made Driftwood want to cry. All the work that she had accomplished suddenly seemed pointlessly insignificant. She wanted to tell them that her magic could only do so much. She wanted to say that she was trying her best. She wanted to get mad at others who weren't. Instead she just closed her eyes and held back her tears.

Is this what it would have felt like to be cruelly teased? wondered Driftwood who had never gone to school and had grown up without any other children around her. *I don't like it. It's making me feel ashamed of myself. There's too much pressure in the public eye.*

While Driftwood withdrew and Rose defended herself with sarcasm they were rescued by their good friends. Tide, Glacier and Lichen had quickly ridden in from the camp. Using horses and volleyball nets they scurried the reporters away, all the while making sure not to hurt them.

"Remember that they're just trying to make a living," Swamp the camp director had advised the trio before they had left the stables.

Tide hoisted Driftwood up onto his horse while Rose joined Lichen. Driftwood felt nervous when she put her hands around his waist. Things had felt so comfortable when they had spoken on the phone but they were both suddenly ridiculously awkward. Tide's voice cracked when he spoke.

"Stormy…eik…went home to his… uh…mother," he managed to say. "So…uh… how…uh…was your trip?"

"It was…um…OK…uh…but…ei…not really," returned Driftwood. "You know… um…we almost got…uh…blown up…but… well…you know."

"Yeah."

"Yeah."

"Sooooo."

"I didn't hang up on you."

CHAPTER FOURTEEN

"Pardon me?"

"I didn't hang up on you, Tide. The phone cut off, probably because of my blasted father."

"That's cool."

"Yeah?"

"Yeah."

Anytime with Tide had become inexplicably exciting for Driftwood. The energy between the two of them eventually started to relax, flutter and flourish.

"You know, Witch-ster, I can't come out here all the time to rescue you," Tide joked.

"Boyo, you think scaring away some reporters is the same as quelling the violent impulses of old gods?"

"I could always take you back there for more questions."

"My hero," flirted Driftwood.

They enjoyed the rest of the ride. Driftwood talked about growing up on Ellesmere Island. Tide shared stories from his home on Prince Edward Island.

Just as the group had finished unsaddling the horses did the school bus finally arrive. It was a group of school kids from Cypress Mountain Girls School coming for a week of science and outdoor education. The counselors all ran out to greet the newcomers.

As the second girl got off the bus she suddenly kicked the girl in front of her. She had a Driftwood action figure in her hand.

"I'm Driftwood with my Ninja-Kick," she hissed as she tried to kick the girl behind her.

"Holy Ma-Joley," commented Rose.

Suddenly, two more girls were coming off the bus pulling each other's hair. They were also each holding onto a Rose doll with their free hand.

"I look more like Rose!" screamed one.

"No, I do!" asserted the other.

"Whoa Nelly," continued Rose. "This is too weird."

CHAPTER SEVENTEEN

DIALOGUE WITH A RED SQUIRREL

When Driftwood had worked at Camp Magee during the previous summer, she had established one particular spot in the forest as her *special place*. It was here that she could go sit and quietly be with only herself and nature. It had been a place for meditative reflection as well as solace from the barrage of noise and activity that constantly being around kids ensured.

After the scene at the bus, Driftwood quickly retreated to her *special place* to ruminate on her predicament. She had inadvertently signed over the license to her image to her father's company. Driftwood had hoped that by mass-marketing herself she could more greatly influence children to care about the world's problems with the same intensity that she did. Instead, GBP had created toys that brought out violence and vanity in the first few kids that she had seen playing with them. It was very distressing and she felt a horrible amount of shame and guilt. She started to cry. Over her own wails she could hear a strange nibbling sound.

She wiped her eyes, looked up and was greeted by a disturbing site. It front of her was a red squirrel holding a Driftwood action figure in its mouth. The doll, now riddled with scratches and divots, was about the same size as the squirrel.

"Are you a goddess?" asked the squirrel as it dropped the toy and jumped to a branch that was near the real Driftwood's face.

"Not at all," huffed Driftwood,

remembering that Sedna had given her the ability to talk to animals. "In fact, I feel very powerless."

"With all of these idols of you that have shown up," remarked the squirrel, "someone must worship you."

"More like curse me. My father has exploited my persona and now girls are kicking each other."

"That's because of you? I was wondering what was up. The human kids who are around here are usually so happy and generally kind to each other."

"Are you the squirrel god that has been gossiping about me?"

"I wish," replied the red squirrel, "but I'm no god. In fact, squirrel gods are not even truly squirrels."

"What are they?" inquired Driftwood.

"When any squirrel gathers a pine cone and stores it for the leaner months, it is helping create squirrel gods. Every midden of seeds made and each nest that is constructed gives our gods strength. The squirrel gods are our labour."

"That's cool," remarked the young mage. "It's kind of like how Silla isn't really an Inuit god of air and weather. Silla really is more like the wind and rain itself."

"Who's Silla?"

"Nevermind. So your gods come from you and your kind than the other way around?"

"I guess. I never thought about it much. I will most likely only live for three turns of the seasons and I've already seen more than two. Stories of the squirrel gods entertain me, teach me and motivate me to gather cones during my short term on this planet. Also, the squirrel gods gives me someone to thank and blame."

"Blame?"

"It's better than blaming oneself when things don't go right."

"Why do we have to blame anyone when something is wrong? Why can't we just focus on fixing the problem?"

"Aren't you holding your father at fault for making you into a false goddess?"

"That's not the point. In fact, blame seems pointless when it doesn't solve anything and there's so much to do."

"And what are you going to do?"

"Before I can focus on the world's pressing problems I'm going to stop the distribution of those annoying Driftwood and Rose toys."

"How?"

"We'll see," stated Driftwood as she stood up and marched back to the camp with determination. Now all she needed was a plan.

As she entered the open field Rose ran up to greet her.

"You won't believe this," informed Rose, "but someone just called the camp and left an anonymous message telling us where the dolls are being produced. The first freight leaves tomorrow from your father's Shanghai factory on route to North America."

"It could be a trap," contemplated

Driftwood.

"It could be someone on the inside is helping us."

"It doesn't matter."

"Why not?"

"I'm not afraid of my father's traps."

CHAPTER EIGHTEEN

PLAYING CARDS WITH THE COSMOS

Jupiter is about five times further from the Sun than Earth. Orbiting this gaseous planet is Callisto, a giant spherical rock that has had no geological activity in over four billion years. On this long dead moon a tense game amongst eternal beings was being played. Sitting at a poker table were Artemis, the Greek goddess of wilderness; Freya, Norse leader of the mythical Valkyrie; Elvis Presley, legendary god-king of rock and roll and the

On this long dead moon a tense game amongst eternal beings was being played.

mighty Squamish Thunderbird of Native American lore.

The gods and goddesses were having a leisurely game while using the gathering as an opportunity to gamble for news.

"I have two pair, queen high," stated Artemis as she laid down her cards.

"Three of a kind," revealed Freya as she showed a trio of eights to her adversaries.

"Dang a lang, y'all," sighed Elvis. "All I have is a pair of kings. What about you, Thund-ster?"

"Ka-ka! I almost have a flush," responded the Native American bird-god. "Does that count for anything?"

Freya had won the hand.

"Well, pay up," the love goddess insisted. "Information from all of you."

"Due to the influence of Driftwood Ellesmere, Odin and his sons are wandering North America battling corporate giants," provided Artemis playfully. "Loki is with them."

"Please tell me something I don't know, Elvis, as Artemis seems to think that giving me facts about my fellow Norse is worth something," Freya complained.

"The Blekansits have made a plastic icon of Driftwood," informed Mr. Presley, "that ain't as good as my doll with the specially designed swivel hips. Hubba hubba hubba."

"I am astounded," responded Freya, "at how powerful that mortal girl is getting without really desiring it."

Suddenly, the Thunderbird shot up and stared toward Earth.

"Speaking of which," the mystical bird revealed as it extended its wings, "I am just now being called by Driftwood to take her to Shanghai so she can stop the first shipment of her toy figures. Excuse me, friends, and thank you for the game. Ka-ka!"

"Very interesting," considered Freya as she watched her fellow immortal fly off into space.

Chapter Nineteen

A Ship of Foolish Toys

"Is the wind always this bad when you travel, Rose?" asked Tide as he tried to speak over the rushing gales.

"Going by cloud was a bit tamer," confessed Rose, "but the Thunderbird is very fast."

"Don't you find it strange that its feet have lizard faces on them?"

"Tide, when you've hung out with Drifty as much as I have, strange is one of the few constants. Besides, the lizards are omens of security."

Tide had decided to join Driftwood and Rose on their quest. The trio was being flown across the world by the messenger god of the Squamish Nation. Driftwood was silent during the whole journey. She was nervous about Tide being with them. Her concern for his safety was one reason. The fact that she often got a little sick to her stomach when talking to him was another. She was also extremely uneasy about where they were going.

When Driftwood had last been to China, she had tried to free young girls from making toys for Great Blekansit Products. Even after she and Rose had rendered all the guards of her father's factory powerless the young workers still did not flee. In order to help their families they had chosen to stay to work in the factory's horrible conditions for meager pay. The complexity of the situation had anguished the young sorceress considerably. Her memories certainly distracted her when they arrived at the GBP Shanghai factory.

In the harbour was a giant cargo ship that was loading crates from the warehouse of the sweatshop. Helena, Hans and Harry Blekansit were standing with the ship's captain on the deck of the boat. Hans was yelling and frantically waving his arms in the air. The captain looked quite scared.

"Are you saying," screamed Hans, "that you won't be able to get the units out to the east coast until next Friday? We've already planned a nationwide media blitz for this weekend and won't be able to capitalize on our prime impulse buying window! Who's to blame for this?"

"Maybe no one is to blame," a voice interrupted. "Maybe it's part of just everything happening."

Hans could suddenly feel a burst of air blow against his bald head. He looked behind him to see a giant, abstractly shaped bird, lowering his daughter and two of her annoying friends onto the deck.

"For the record, Father, I don't want to blame you for all you do and have done," continued Driftwood. "I just want to stop you from doing it anymore."

"You are just the hardest daughter to kill," complained Hans. "How did you know to find us here?"

"I was tipped off."

Hans' face turned red, Helena looked shocked and Harry studied the laces of his wingtip shoes.

But only the three of us knew we were coming here, contemplated Hans as he looked over at Harry and recognized his son's look of guilt.

"You stupid boy, how could you?" asked Hans angrily.

"I was watching the news on TV and saw Driftwood after she had been rescued," explained the betraying son. "Everyone wanted to talk to her and she hadn't even tried and didn't even care about getting the recognition. All I've ever wanted was your attention, Father. All I have ever desired was your love and care,

Mother, so your longtime absence made me angry. And Father encouraged me to act on that anger. As I watched Driftwood meditate in front of the reporters I had a significant revelation. I needed to free myself of my desire for my parents' approval and caring so that I could care about the whole world. After I understood that, it was easy to decide what to do. I called the camp and told them we were flying here because I think Driftwood's right. You have to be stopped."

Harry moved over and stood beside his half-sister and her friends.

Wow, thought Driftwood, *my brother may not be so annoying after all.*

"I am furious with both of you children!" bellowed Hans.

"Not only are you furious," Driftwood incanted as her hand gracefully danced in the air, "but you're also a penguin."

Driftwood was hoping that she would be able to change Hans in a way similar to when she had turned him into a rabbit.

"Oh no, he's not," responded Helena with a wave of her arm.

Nothing happened to Hans.

"And you say you don't love me, Helena," mused Hans.

"I've been practicing magic since before you were born, stepdaughter. Anything you can do I can do better."

"We'll see about that," Driftwood boldly stated as she pulled out her Mason jar. She started to unlatch and open the lid so she could sprinkle some pocket lint and pour some raspberry juice into the container.

Helena swirled her fingers around in front of her face. She began to chant:

Oh powers of the unknown
Fueled by my husband's rage
Turn his daughter's tool
From jar into a cage

The Mason jar suddenly grew and engulfed Driftwood, Rose, Tide and Harry. The four started banging on each of the walls but to no avail. Driftwood realized that she was now trapped in her own magical instrument.

"Holy Ma-Joley!" exclaimed Rose

"How accurate, Rose," explained Helena, "as first we'll start with holes."

Instantly, little cork-shaped pieces of glass started to pop off of the various sides of the jar. There were suddenly numerous finger-size holes all over the cylindrical prison.

"And then you'll roll," continued the sorceress as her fingers twirled about.

The jar tipped onto its side and started to turn over and over. It fell off the edge of the deck as the quartet of kids were tossed around inside. Tide accidentally elbowed Driftwood in the face as Rose's foot went into Harry's stomach. There was a big splash. The permeable jar quickly filled with water as it started to sink into the ocean.

"And soon you'll drown," finished Helena.

CHAPTER TWENTY

SQUID PRO QUO

"We're all going to die!" screamed Harry.

"Uh, Drifty?" inquired Rose as she tried to remain calm.

"Can you do anything?" asked Tide.

"Jar disappear," Driftwood chanted calmly as she waved her hand.

Nothing happened.

"That witch!" yelled Driftwood. "She's turned my own stuff against me! First she misrepresents my image and now this!"

"We'll get her later, Drifty," assured Rose,

"but right now we have our impending doom to prevent."

They had sunk a great deal into the depths of the ocean. The jar was almost completely full of water. There was very little oxygen to breathe. Driftwood closed her eyes and started to whisper a magic spell.

Skoo wop a doo hop
Bing a bang a bice
Make the water 'round us
Change right into ice

Suddenly, the water around the outside of the glass started to freeze. A thick sheet of ice started to cover the jar. This prevented anymore water from coming in. As well, because ice is less dense than water, they started to float up.

"You did it, Driftwood!" yelled Tide.

"We're rising, confirmed Rose, "and we can breathe. Good thinking."

"We're saved," sighed a relieved Harry.

Moments later, the jar was prevented from continuing its upward trajectory. Eight massive tentacles wrapped around the capsule of glass and ice. The group was suddenly in the clutches of a giant squid. The oceanic leviathan started to pull the jar back into the abyss of the dark and deep waters. The frosty shield started to melt.

"We're all going to die!" cried Harry whose panicky outbursts were starting to annoy his half-sister.

However, as the squid pulled their craft ever downward, Driftwood began to suspect that Harry was correct. Things did not look good. She contemplated their fate and tried to come up with a plan.

"Uh…Driftwood," interrupted Tide, "there's been something I've been meaning to tell you and…uh…because we're going to die and all that…um…I want you to know…"

BUMP!

Tide was interrupted by a massive change in their movement.

What now? thought Driftwood. *Tide was about to tell me something important just before we die. It felt very romantic.*

BUMP!

"Look outside!" enthused Rose. "We really might be saved!"

As the four gathered their wits and looked through the ice and glass, they could see a whale banging its head against the squid.

BUMP!

The squid finally released its prey. In mere moments, the jar started to rise up again, this time with the aid of two other whales. As quickly as they reached the surface had the ice almost completely melted away. Greeting them was Tyr and the whale that Driftwood had saved in the Norwegian Sea. Tyr was still holding strong to the whale's tail-fin. Tyr struck the jar with his handless arm and smashed off the lid. Four heads quickly bobbed out gasping for fresh air.

"Thank you very much for your rescue," greeted Driftwood although she was a bit miffed that she didn't hear what Tide had to say.

"One good turn deserves another," mused the whale.

"How did you know to find us here?"

"Freya of the Norse Æsir and leader of the Valkyrie advised me of your situation," explained Tyr. "It appears you have awoken a desire amongst her and her fellow women warriors to rise from their slumber and rejoin the mortal world."

Driftwood looked up and saw what looked like a flock of birds fly out from inside a cloud. She could soon see that it wasn't birds at all. Leading a charge was Freya in a chariot being pulled by giant cats. Behind her were twelve other women clad in armour and helmets brandishing swords, axes and shields and riding mighty flying steeds. Within moments they began to attack both the ship and the toy plant. There soon were guards thwarted, crates smashed and mechanisms disabled amidst a storm of smoke and fury.

"Holy Ma-Joley," muttered Driftwood.

"Took the words right out of my mouth," concurred Rose, "because it definitely looks like the cavalry has arrived."

Chapter Twenty-One

The Final Battle Ride of the Valkyrie

The factory guard had never seen a Valkyrie before. He did not know that shooting at her would only serve to make her angry. The bullets deflected off of Randgrid's shield as she responded quickly with a slice of her sword. The guard watched as the barrel of his gun slid off of its handle. He ran away screaming.

A cloud of wooden and plastic splinters exploded from each strike of Skeggjöld's axe. The crates of toys were no match for her mighty blows.

Inside the factory was a complicated machine that used a variety of interlinked gears and presses to cover each action figure with a casing of clear plastic and coloured cardboard. The placing of Geirölul's spear between two gears was enough to cause the system to buckle and collapse in on itself. Suddenly, the ten-year-old workers had no packaged toys to load into boxes.

"No longer shall you work like slaves," promised Geirölul the Valkyrie as smoke began to emit from the machine.

Back on the boat's deck, Hans and Helena were hastily getting into their helicopter. The propellers began to turn rapidly as the pair quickly flew off.

Foiled by my daughter yet again, thought Hans. *One day I shall have my revenge.*

Driftwood has the power of the Valkyrie on her side, thought Helena. *Interesting.*

Driftwood, Rose, Tide and Harry were climbing out of the giant jar and onto the

"No longer shall you work like slaves."

dock next to the factory. As they tried to wring the water out of their clothes they watched as thirteen women warriors flew around and landed in front of the quartet. They were all on powerful horses except for Freya who road a chariot pulled by cats. She disembarked and approached Driftwood.

"Well, I don't know who you are," greeted Driftwood, "but you sure know how to make an entrance."

"I am Freya, Norse leader of the Valkyrie, and I have been following your career for quite some time."

"Yeah, I know how you goddesses like to gossip," quipped Driftwood.

"It is not gossip," defended Freya. "It is information that we use to help make decisions. Much like how your recent actions have influenced the Valkyrie to make our biggest choice in almost a millennium."

"And what is that?"

"In the past days of Asgard we were powerful spirits who dictated who lived or died in battle. It was a very specific role in the pantheon of the Norse. We eventually tired of it and slumbered for many a generation. However, tales of your exploits have awoken my sisters. We seek to re-enter the world and not be relegated to such a singular and military purpose. I intend to enter the world of politics to affect the systems of governing."

The other Valkyrie each took turns introducing themselves to Driftwood.

"I am Skeggjöld of the Axe-Age and I shall turn my skills with the blade towards becoming a surgeon to aid the injured and ailing."

"I am Mist of the Cloud and I hope to become an air scientist in hopes of rescuing our atmosphere from the ravages of pollution."

"I am Geirölul the Spear-Waver and I will pursue beauty and grace as a rhythmic gymnast."

"I am Rádgríd of the Counsel-Truce and I will become a diplomat who seeks peace amongst nations."

"I am Herfjötur the Host-fetter and I will become a philosopher who seeks to discover the truth behind all things."

"I am Hlökk of Noise and I intend to liberate the masses from their societal illusions as a punk rock singer."

"I am Randgrid of the Shield-Truce and I plan to become a peace activist."

"I am Reginleif of the Power-Trace and I will seek to investigate and understand the past as a professor of history."

"I am Skögul the Shaker and I will become a hippy dancer of the unending love generation, spreading joy with my motions and movements."

"I am Göll of the Tumultuous Times and I want to help others with their conflicts as a family counselor."

"I am Thrúd of the Power and I want to become a teacher. In fact, my first students will be the children of this factory."

"And I am Hild of the Battle. I will become a business woman. My initial plan is to change this factory so that it will treat its employees fairly and only hire workers of an adult age."

"How can you do that?" asked Driftwood. "It's owned by my father."

"Not anymore," replied Hild as she brought out a sheet of paper from behind her shield. "Hans Blekansit accidentally sold it to me when he thought he was selling his first shipment of Driftwood toys. He also gave me the rights to your images which I will return to you girls. I guess he forgot to read the fine print."

Rose was impressed as she looked at the thirteen Valkyries who stood in front of them.

"Wow, Drifty," she quipped, "and you were worried about your personal message not getting out. Now, here you are, influencing goddesses to help save the world."

Chapter Twenty-Two

Dénouement

"Goodbye, Tyr," waved Driftwood. "Keep saving those whales."

Driftwood and her friends watched as the whales dove into the ocean with Tyr still holding tight to the tail-fin of his comrade of the deep.

Harry and Rose started talking to some Valkyries. Driftwood suddenly found herself walking alone with Tide. Her nerves began to act up. Fortunately, he started to speak.

"Uh, Driftwood?"

"Yeah, Tide?"

"You know, I think you're really awesome and you've done all these great things and I really like being with you…"

He stopped for a moment. Driftwood couldn't help but get excited from hearing the barrage of compliments. She listened intently as Tide continued.

"…but I need to go home to Fairfield to be with my family."

Dang, thought Driftwood.

"What's wrong?" she asked aloud doing all she could to hide her frustration.

"I had called home to my family just before we left camp. My father's fishing business has gone under," explained the boy, "and I have to go help them figure out what to do next, as jobs are scarce in Prince Edward Island. I'm catching a ride with Hlökk who is on her way to Nova Scotia to be part of the Halifax punk scene."

Driftwood thought about offering to summon some god-being that would take them both wherever they needed to go but shyly resisted. That might have come off as too forward. As well, she was already a bit overwhelmed with the high number of deities that she had encountered as of late. Dealing with the personalities of such mighty entities was mentally exhausting. Having almost just drowned caused great physical fatigue. She wished she could just fly home from China in an airplane but she didn't have a passport or any money for that matter. The whining of her half-brother distracted her from her own tiredness.

"What will I do?" squealed Harry. "I've betrayed my father! I have no place to eat or sleep!"

"Take it easy," comforted Rose. "I'm pretty sure we can find a job for you at Camp Magee."

"Aren't you the girl who made me fart for a month?"

"And now I'm one of your only friends. The world's funny that way. So, let's ride,

Stinky."

Harry and Rose hitched with Skeggjöld and Skögul who were traveling to San Francisco to become a doctor and a dancer, respectively. As Rose was getting on Skeggjöld's horse she called out to her best friend.

"Hey, Drifty! Are you coming along to camp?"

"I need to go to Ellesmere Island first! I'll see you there later."

"I can give you passage in my carrier," offered the Valkyrie queen.

Driftwood studied the ornate and elegant wagon that was connected to two fantastically large felines. She stepped onto the chariot and waved goodbye to her friends. She, Freya and the cats flew into the air.

"What are you thinking, mortal?" the goddess asked after a few minutes of silence.

"Right now, I'm just trying not to think."

"What do you mean?"

"I'm just trying not to think about Tide

with his arms around the waist of that Valkyrie as they soar across the world. That's all."

"Ah, love is a difficult but worthwhile path, young girl," comforted Freya.

"I never said I loved him," corrected Driftwood. "I just like him a bit. That's all."

"As you say. So, little one, information on you is always a valued commodity to bring to poker games. Can you tell me what plans you have next?"

"Well, let's stop at my igloo in Aujuittuq to pick up Edie my pet Eaderion. Then, I want to catch up to Rose and Harry at Camp Magee as I've realized something vital. I think I know the most reliable way to help the world and have fun while doing it."

"And what is that?"

"I'm going to go play with kids."

THE END

The Creators

JAMES DAVIDGE, AUTHOR, is a teacher in Alberta. He is moving to the country and looks forward to racing twigs down the creek.

ERIC JORDAN, INTERIOR ILLUSTRATIONS, is a civil engineer from Nova Scotia. Before that he helped defend a summer camp from a variety of evil-doers.

FIONA STAPLES, COVER AND BOOK DESIGN, is normally a comic book artist but is also fond of real books.